RICK BRICK

AND THE QUEST TO

SAVE BRICKPORT

RICK BRICK
AND THE QUEST TO
SAVE BRICKPORT

An Unofficial LEGO Novel

TAMONY HALL

Sky Pony Press
New York

Sky Pony Press books may be purchased in bulk at special discounts for sales promotion, corporate gifts, fund-raising, or educational purposes. Special editions can also be created to specifications. For details, contact the Special Sales Department, Sky Pony Press, 307 West 36th Street, 11th Floor, New York, NY 10018 or info@skyhorsepublishing. com.

Sky Pony˙ is a registered trademark of Skyhorse Publishing, Inc.˙, a Delaware corporation.

Visit our website at www.skyponypress.com.

10 9 8 7 6 5 4 3 2 1

Library of Congress Cataloging-in-Publication Data is available on file.

Special thanks to Tamson Weston.

Cover design by Gretchen Schuyler
Cover illustration credit: Matt Armstrong

Print ISBN: 978-1-63450-149-1
Ebook ISBN: 978-1-63450-923-7

Printed in Canada

CONTENTS

RICK BRICK

AND THE QUEST TO

SAVE BRICKPORT

CHAPTER ONE
TROUBLE IN BRICKPORT

Rick watched the Ferris wheel turn above him, the highest point rising up over the water with a clear view all the way to the open ocean, just as he had planned it. He could hear the gleeful screams of the passengers as he arranged the final colorful bricks in the mosaic he was working on just below their feet.

"Beautiful work, Rick," said the mayor. He looked up to see her smiling over him. But then, out of nowhere, a siren blared. But it wasn't a siren, really. It sounded more like a horn or a loud truck backing up. In fact, the more closely Rick listened, the more he noticed it sounded exactly like . . . his alarm clock.

Rick rolled off his squat brick bed and landed face first on the studded floor. It had all been a lovely dream. Had Rick not fallen out of bed, he might have stayed in his perfect dream world all day. As it was, he was tempted to remain on the floor. When he finally pulled himself to his feet, he tripped over his briefcase on the way to the bathroom. His toothbrush was stuck in the rack, and as he yanked it out, he knocked his favorite razor into the toilet. Luckily, Rick didn't have much use for the razor. His face was always shiny and smooth, whether he shaved or not.

Rick brushed his teeth vigorously. His expression might have been as cheerful as usual, but his spirits were low. He had a meeting with his partner, Rita, that he was not looking forward to. Business was bad at Brick and Block Builders, the company he and Rita co-owned. The town of Brickport was almost bankrupt and no one wanted new buildings anymore. With a heavy sigh, Rick wiped toothpaste from his mouth with his pajama sleeve and went to the bedroom to get dressed.

Putting on his shoes took longer than usual—he couldn't get them to click into place. Rick was nearly out the door before he realized he'd snapped his shirt on backwards. Thankfully, he was having a good hair day—but then every day was a good hair day in Brickport. Even when everything else was falling apart, you could still count on your hair to be perfect. With a deep breath, Rick picked up his briefcase and headed out the door.

He wandered down Pegg Street toward Rotor Boulevard. As he turned the corner, he tripped over the edge of a sidewalk baseplate and slid several feet on his stomach.

"Blasted sidewalk!" yelled Rick, to no one in particular.

Rick tripped in a different spot on his walk almost every day. The flat gray bricks and slabs that made up the sidewalks in Brickport never matched or fit together properly. Some of them weren't even locked onto other bricks. One misstep could send a whole piece spinning across the street. Many of the studs on the sidewalk blocks were worn off completely. It made the hills even more difficult to climb.

The buildings that lined the sidewalks were in no better shape. Most of them couldn't even be called buildings—they had fallen completely apart or had been picked apart so that they were more space than brick. Two-by-twos and two-by-fours had been pulled out of the middle of walls. Corner bricks were missing on many buildings. Even the structures that were still standing and intact were depressing to look at. Many of them had been put up fast to make a quick buck, and now they sat empty. Odd-shaped pieces from various sets were crammed together haphazardly—because the right bricks weren't available—and none of the colors matched. Everything was being gradually picked apart. Rick wondered if he might just walk outside one day and find nothing but piles of odd-shaped pieces that were of no use to anyone. The thought made him sad. He liked to think that most bricks had a job, that there was at least one place for every brick.

Rick turned toward the harbor. It took a little longer to get to work that way, but he liked the walk better. Boats still came to the port, even though there weren't quite as many of them. There weren't nearly as many recreational boats as there once were—they had sailed for bluer seas. The parks were covered with garbage and broken equipment, but there were still green baseplates here and there, and clusters of plants and flowers that some of the residents had attached to help cheer things up—without help from the city. There was hope, if you were willing to look for it. It was hard for Rick to give up on Brickport. It had always been his home, and he loved it.

Rick turned right at the corner and headed toward Starbricks. There was a scuffle in front of the entrance. Three young men were teasing a scruffy old man wearing a battered trench coat and a captain's hat.

"Nice hat, Cap'n. How much you want for it?" said the biggest boy in the group. "Nothing? Good!" He held the cap in the air, just out of the old man's reach.

"Hey! Hey! *Leave him alone!*" Rick shouted. He tried to look as intimidating as possible. The boys turned toward him, shocked.

"Oh, you want the hat, Mr. Tough Guy?" the leader said. "Catch!"

Rick reached out with both hands and dropped his briefcase.

"That's a good trade!" said the smallest boy. He grabbed the case and bolted. His friends followed.

Rick didn't bother to chase them. "Aw, what's the use," he said. He handed the old man his hat. "Here you go, Stan. I can't imagine you without this."

Stan was an old friend. Rick usually ran into him a couple times a week and stopped to chat and share a cup of coffee. The old guy was a lot like Brickport. His shoes were worn and his coat was threadbare, but behind his rough exterior was a different story. Rick liked talking to Stan because Stan knew about the old Brickport. Like Rick, Stan still had hope that the city could return to its former glory. But that hope slowly faded with every missing brick.

"Buy you a coffee?" Rick asked.

"Why, thank you, Rick. That's mighty kind of you," Stan replied.

They said the same thing every time they met. And then they talked about the news and the state of Brickport. Usually Rick played the part of the cheerleader. He always had big ideas to share. But this was the worst morning in a string of bad mornings, and Rick just wasn't up for a pep talk today.

"Haven't heard much from the mayor lately," said Stan.

"Ah, she's just like every other crooked politician," Rick replied. "City of Dreams my foot. She never had any intention of building that community center."

"Rick! That doesn't sound like you!" said Stan.

"I'm sorry, Stan, but that's how I feel," Rick said. He sighed deeply.

"Something eating you? Out with it!" said Stan.

"Rita and I are meeting at the office this morning to discuss business. We've been avoiding talking about it, but now I think it's time to face the music. We're gonna have to close down Brick and Block."

"That *is* bad news . . . I'm sorry to hear it," said Stan.

"Thanks, Stan," Rick said. "It's a tough call, but no new jobs have come in for a while. No one cares about Brickport anymore . . . except us, of course."

"Isn't there something I can do?" Stan asked.

"I don't think so, Stan. Just keep having coffee with me . . . and reminding me what's good about Brickport," said Rick.

"I'd be happy to," said Stan.

"Well, I better get going," said Rick.

"Try to cheer up," called Stan. "The answer may be right around the corner."

◄◦►

Rick had thought things might change after the last election. Mayor Minn E. Figg had promised to clean up the town, beginning with the port. She had also promised to build a community center with parks and gardens and little shops and offices for the city's residents. But after an initial flurry of speeches and public appearances, Mayor Figg had all but disappeared. In fact, Rick couldn't remember the last time he'd heard the mayor speak. She always sent someone else to speak for her—someone who managed to answer questions without *really* answering them.

Rick took a left and headed back toward the port. It would take a little longer, but he was in no hurry to face bad news. Besides, he wanted to pass one of his favorite places in Brickport.

An old band shell faced out toward the harbor. Like everything else in town, pieces of the structure had been scavenged so that it wasn't even quite a shell anymore. What should have been a smooth stretch of gray was interrupted with divots and holes where plates and bricks had been pulled away. Most of the seats were missing, too. But just next to the band shell was a semicircle of trees and a wide, green field—or mostly green, anyway. Kids still gathered there occasionally to play soccer or to ride skateboards.

Even now, a group of street dancers gathered at the center of the band shell. Rick stopped to watch them. The park wasn't really so bad. A new green baseplate or two could be brought in to fill the holes in the field, and some gray tiles and new seats would do the trick for the band shell. The loose bricks just needed to be collected and placed where they once were. Rick could picture plays and concerts being performed there once again. It was a perfect place for children to play and for family and friends to gather. The trees seemed to demand that picnic blankets be spread beneath them. It was a wonder they hadn't been removed from the base or had their branches pulled out yet.

Rick continued walking with a final, sad look over his shoulder. He turned right on Angle Avenue toward Brick and Block Associates, the architecture and building firm he shared with his partner, Rita. He paused for a moment, studying the letters on the window. He had been so happy and full of hope the day they were stenciled. He and Rita had taken such pains to choose the right colors. Finally, Rick took a deep breath, fixed his hand on the door handle, and pushed it open.

"How bad is it, Rita?" Rick asked, cutting to the chase. But Rita wasn't alone. There, at the modest round conference table, sat an imposing figure in a dark suit. He had serious eyebrows and silly orange hair with a big round puff on the top. Beside him on the table lay a pair of white gloves. It had been so long since anyone but Rita or Rick had entered the office that Rick didn't even know what to do at first. Could this be a new client? Or was it a bill collector?

"Good afternoon, Mr. Brick," said the man. "Nice of you to join us."

"Oh, uh . . . " Rick looked at his watch. "It's only nine a.m. I wasn't expecting . . ."

"I suppose I'll have to start again. I'm Dr. Francis Dubloon. I want to restore our fair city—"

"—to its former glory," Rita said, finishing Dr. Dubloon's sentence. She had clearly heard it already.

"Ahem. Yes, precisely," he continued. "And if we are through with the interruptions, I'd like to ask for your assistance in doing so."

"Well, as I was saying just a minute ago, Dr. Dubloon," said Rita, "Rick and I . . ."

"Yes, yes, Miss Block. I'm sure you're quite helpful," said the doctor. "But I'm really looking for an architect who recalls those days of yore in Brickport. Before the riff-raff started stealing all the best bricks from our finest structures. Also, I understand you're very *well-loved* in the community, Brick—is that right?"

"This is my city, Dr. Dubloon. I love it, and it loves me," Rick said with as much confidence as he could muster.

"Good, good. And all your paperwork is in order, I presume? Proper licenses for building and so forth."

"Uh, yes, of course," Rick answered.

"Wonderful. Let's get down to business then, shall we?" said Dr. Dubloon, tossing a heavy instruction book on the table.

CHAPTER TWO
THE ANSWER TO BRICKPORT'S PRAYERS?

Rick, Rita, and Dr. Dubloon spent two hours going over the thick instruction book. Dr. Dubloon did most of the talking, but since this was the first time they'd had a client in quite a while, Rick didn't want to mess it up. Plus, just two hours earlier, Rick had been worried about the fate of their business, and now, suddenly, here was a solution! Rita tried to ask a few questions about how the community would be affected by the new building and whether they would present their plan at a town meeting, but Dr. Dubloon waved away her concerns.

Finally, when there was a pause, Rick asked, "Doctor, this is a pretty thorough set of instructions. Nothing's been left out."

"Yes. I'm glad you noticed," Dr. Dubloon said, removing his coffee cup from a nearby stud on the table.

"So," Rick asked, "why do you need us? It seems you have this under control yourself."

"Well, I've had a bit of difficulty getting the proper paperwork in order. You know how troublesome all these rules and regulations can be." Dr. Dubloon waved his hand around, as if at an invisible fly. "The mayor suggested that you might be a good solution to that problem. And the people in Brickport like you, do they not?"

"I like to think so, yes," said Rick.

"Good. We'll need that, too. Is one million dollars enough to get this project started?"

"Uh, geez. Well . . . yes! That should be just fine!" Rick said. He looked over at Rita. She glared back. He wondered if he'd been too hasty, but it was such a big number!

"Rick, can we chat for just a second?" Rita whispered.

"Um . . ." Rick looked around the tiny office. "Would you please excuse us for a moment, Doctor?"

"Over here," Rita said, waving Rick toward the coat closet. They walked inside.

"I don't know about this, Rick. I've got a bad feeling about Dr. Dubloon," Rita said. She looked worried.

"Rita, he may be a bit curt, but he's offering us a million dollars!" Rick almost shouted.

"Shhh! Keep your voice down. This guy could afford twice that. There's just something I don't like about him," Rita whispered.

"I know he's a little odd. But do we have a choice?" Rick asked.

Rita sighed. "I guess not."

They opened the closet door and returned to the conference table.

"You've got a deal, Dr. Dubloon," Rick said, extending his hand.

"Good." Dr. Dubloon put on his gloves. Then he took Rick's hand and shook it firmly. Rick took it back and stuck it to his wrist.

"We're going to take this town into the future, young man," Dr. Dubloon said as he turned to leave.

"Of course. But we'll also be staying true to the way the city once was, right?" Rita asked.

"Sure, sure." Dr. Dubloon brushed Rita's concerns aside with a wave of his hand. It was the same wave he had used to get rid of those pesky rules and regulations from earlier in the meeting. Then he walked out the door.

Suddenly the whole day seemed new.

"Wow! Rita, can you believe it?" Rick said. He was feeling the happiest he'd been in months.

"Well, it's certainly convenient timing, but I . . ."

"Convenient timing? It's just what I've been hoping for!" Rick shouted.

"Sure, the money is good . . . but . . ."

"It's like a dream come true!"

"That's what worries me, Rick."

"Rita, you worry too much. The doctor is weird, but we only have to deal with him for one project. And this could be the beginning of a new day for Brickport," Rick said, sitting back in his chair.

"Yes, you said that, Rick, but look at those instructions. If you were going to build something to revitalize the city, would it be *that* building? It has turrets and a launching pad. It's like the fort you designed when you were a little boy playing war. But Dr. Dubloon is no little boy. He's got money and connections, and he's not playing. What does he want with that building? What about the new parks you've been saying the city should have? What about the community? "

"This *will* help the community, eventually. Look, can't we just enjoy the moment? Just for now? Think of how many problems a million dollars will solve! Why are you so paranoid?" Rick leaned his elbows on the table.

"Yeah, I'm sure you're right. It will be good for the city. I'm going to grab a sandwich. You stay here and enjoy the moment, Rick," Rita said and walked out the door. Rick suspected she didn't mean it.

With Rita gone, Rick let out a sigh. He hated to admit it, but he had an odd feeling about their new client, too. For starters, he didn't like that the building plans all seemed to be so . . . settled. Usually, he and Rita would start with a basic kit and then customize it with their own particular flourishes. That was the fun part—when they dreamed that anything was possible. In fact, most of their clients came to them *for* their flourishes! But for this project, they didn't have anything to do with the planning whatsoever. It was all there in Dr. Dubloon's big instruction book. Rick and Rita would be little more than glorified foremen for this project.

Still, it was business—the only business they'd had in almost a year—so Rick couldn't help but feel grateful . . . and a little excited. Maybe this would be the kick-start the city needed. Rick wanted to think so.

◄○►

The next few weeks were very busy. Rita seemed to have gotten over her concerns enough to get on with the job, although she and Rick hadn't spoken about it again. Rick suspected that the project still didn't sit right with her. He couldn't help thinking she might be on to something as the building got underway.

Rick had held out a faint hope that Dr. Dubloon would choose a spot by the harbor for the Dubloon Tower. Rick liked the idea of working near the water and watching the boats. He also thought that maybe the new building would draw other projects to their company.

"What? Near that horrid decaying port?" said Dr. Dubloon at Rick's suggestion. "Heh, heh. I don't think so, Rick. Do you know how much the taxes are for a lot near the port? And for what? A daily whiff of brackish water? No, no, no. It's going to take a lot of work to clean that place up. You'll see that I've made the right decision about where to build. Besides, you can see everything from here and it will all be mi . . . uh . . . marvelous—simply marvelous—once we turn this place around. Heh, heh."

The building was to be erected right in the center of the city, atop the highest hill. Dubloon was right. You could see everything from there. And it was hard to miss just how bad things had gotten in Brickport. Piles of abandoned specialty bricks sat on every corner of the town, and all the streets had missing baseplates. Almost every sign had been removed from its stud, too, and hardly any of the cars had wheels. Rick hoped Dubloon meant what he said and that this location would help Brickport regain some of its old glory.

At the very least, Rick and Rita had enough money to hire a crew and create some jobs in Brickport—or so Rick thought at first. But when they showed up the first day of work with their crew, Dr. Dubloon was already at the site with a large group of workers. They looked remarkably similar and dressed exactly the same—in black coveralls and matching hats. They also didn't seem very healthy; they were all a bit pale and dead-eyed.

"Oh, Dr. Dubloon, we've got our crew already. They're all very hard workers. Rita and I . . ." Rick began to say.

"Not necessary, Brick. I've got your, uh, men here. I prefer to use them," Dr. Dubloon said, pointing at his crew.

"But Dr. Dubloon, citizens of Brickport are counting on the work," Rick pleaded.

Dr. Dubloon sighed heavily. "All right, Rick!" He grabbed a fistful of gold coins from his pocket and tossed them at Rick's crew.

"There you are. Be on your way now. Skedaddle," he called to Rick's crew. The workers wandered away, looking confused and hurt. Dubloon turned to Rick. "Problem solved, Brick. Okay? Now we can all get to work. We're on a tight schedule."

Rick looked at Rita, who simply raised her eyebrows and said nothing.

◄○►

The materials for the building, while not exactly to Rick and Rita's taste, were, at least, all color-coordinated. Neither Rick nor Rita had seen so many uniformly colored bricks in years. Unfortunately, they were all black or gray. Still, most of the kits Rita and Rick had used recently had been missing parts. There were pieces that were always hard to come by or so small that they were easily lost and hard to get replacements for. Rita and Rick had always made do with what they could cobble together—usually lots of four-by-twos in primary colors. While Dubloon's plans were, well, boring, and the color scheme was stark, he *had* managed to get all the right pieces gathered. There were bricks of all proportions and sizes: bricks with holes to add extra dowels where they would be needed; angled pieces for odd corners; and plenty of one-by-ones, plates, and tiles. There was a place for every brick, and every brick had a job to do. However, whenever Rick tried to suggest a flourish of his own—an atrium at the entrance, a courtyard with a fountain, or a skylight—Dubloon wouldn't hear of it.

About a month from completion, before everything had been shored up, Rick tried one more time to add his two cents in terms of design. He thought it might be nice to have a space near the entrance to the building where Brickport's residents could see the history of their city as it was in its earlier, grander days. It wouldn't take much—just a little display case. What better place to educate the public about Brickport than here at the Dubloon Tower, where its rebirth would begin?

"Listen, Brick, I'm paying you, aren't I?" Dr. Dubloon said after Rick made his suggestion.

"Well, yes, of course, Doctor. But it's just that I am an architect. Usually I get paid to—" Rick was cut off mid-sentence.

"Yes, but that's the beauty of it! The hard part's been done for you. Now you just have to follow the directions, sign the proper forms, and come to work with a smile. There will be time enough for you to flex your creative muscle once we bring this city back to its old glory. For now, please: Stick. To. The. Plan."

Rick could feel Rita's probing eyes on him from where she stood, directing the crew to Step 114a in the instruction book. She was kind enough to look away when he glanced at her in embarrassment.

It seemed that Rick and Rita were not the only ones with concerns about the new building. Despite what the mayor's spokesperson told them, the citizens didn't have a lot of faith in Dubloon's tower. The people who thought they would have jobs were still jobless, and it didn't seem as though the new building would include any of the things people had been asking for—no places for the community to assemble, nothing to draw in new business, no playgrounds, no shops, no cafés. It was hard to tell just why the tower was being built and whom it would benefit.

Every day, Rick and Rita had to find a new way to enter the building site. A mob of citizens outside the site grew bigger by the day. People carried signs that read: GIVE BACK BRICKPORT; MORE JOBS FEWER SLOBS!; DUBLOON IS DUMB!; and I'M ANGRY SO I MADE THIS SIGN! Dubloon tossed coins off to the side—away from the front of the tower—to clear a path through the mob every morning. The workers had erected a barrier to keep the people of Brickport out of the construction area. Also, Dubloon had insisted that Rick and Rita post signs for Brick and Block Associates around the area with the hope that the community would embrace the project if it came from someone they trusted. It all made Rick uneasy. He didn't want to be associated with this project if it was making the citizens of Brickport mad.

Despite the oddness of their business associate and the angry citizens, the work on the tower itself went smoothly. The workers never complained. They never seemed to eat or go to the bathroom, either. And they weren't good at small talk. In fact, Rick hadn't even managed to learn any of their names, even though he tried hard to make friends with them. At the end of one particularly long shift, he approached the group to say goodnight.

"Thanks for all your hard work today," Rick said to one of Dr. Dubloon's workers.

"Ugh," the worker replied.

"Okay, then, see you tomorrow," Rick said to the guy next to him.

"Blerg," said the worker. Then the workers gradually wandered away with a spooky, spaced-out look in their eyes.

◄○►

The projected finish date was only three weeks away. Rick was getting ready to leave the site one evening when Dr. Dubloon arrived. The billionaire ran his hook-shaped hands lazily over the brickwork.

"It's coming along, isn't it, Doctor?" Rick said.

"Yes, yes, Brick. It's really quite wonderful," Dr. Dubloon said, distantly.

"Oh, absolutely! Your plans were so, uh, thorough. We just have a couple things to finish up. And there's a space in the center slot at the entrance. It seemed like we had all the right pieces at first, but I've checked the inventory pretty thoroughly and we don't have brick 407736b*. We have a 407738, and I have something else from a previous project that's kind of close to the specs. It could work, but the black isn't quite the same and the shape isn't exactly right either."

"Ah, yes. Brick 407736b*. She's a beauty, she is. A very special brick. And no, you won't see her in the inventory. Just don't you worry about that, Rick. I have her in a special place. We can save it for the opening ceremony," Mr. Dubloon said, with a sly smile.

"Okay, then. The opening ceremony. That's in three weeks?" Rick said.

"Well, that's what we originally planned, Brick, but you've done such a bang-up job, I think we'll be ready in a week, don't you?"

"Yes, I guess you're right. A week, then." Rick had a bad feeling all of a sudden.

"You seem a little tired, Brick. Why don't you go home? Get some rest," Dr. Dubloon said.

"I guess I *am* a little tired. Thanks, Doctor. I'll see you tomorrow," Rick said, gathering his things.

"Sure, Brick. Have a pleasant evening."

Rick walked through the door in the barrier, through the mob, and down the hill toward home. He hadn't felt any goodwill in Dubloon's farewell. If anything, he felt slightly chilled. There was something about the way the doctor hooked his hands together. Or the way his pinprick eyes seemed to expand as he stared into the distance at something unseen. Rick would be glad to see that last brick laid and the project completed.

CHAPTER THREE
IN SEARCH OF THE ONYX BRICK

The next day, Rick left the site at the same time as Rita. Since the project began, they had been on slightly different schedules, and today was the first time in a while that they had had an opportunity to really talk. As they walked away from the construction site, they both expressed how relieved they were to be close to finishing the tower.

"So, who's getting employee of the week?" asked Rita. "Blerg or Ugh?"

"I'm holding out for Ooof," said Rick.

Rita laughed. "Listen, Rick, I'm sorry I've been such a party pooper about all of this."

"Forget it, Rita. Let's just finish up the job and move on to better things."

"I'm happy to hear you say that. I've wanted to talk to you, actually. I've got an idea I've been working on."

Just then, Stan appeared in front of them. Rick hadn't seen him since the morning Dr. Dubloon had come into the office.

"Rick, my friend. Tell me you have nothing to do with that monstrosity of a building that's being erected in the center of town," Stan said.

"Uh, well, Stan, as a matter of fact . . ."

"We can talk later, Rick," said Rita. "I'm going to go finish up some paperwork." Rita nodded at Stan, but he didn't notice. She walked away with a wave.

"Rick, please tell me it's not you building that—"

"—monstrosity. Yes, I am building it, Stan. That tower is saving our business and . . ."

"And it's going to RUIN THE WORLD!" Stan yelled.

"Now, that's an exaggeration," Rick said, chuckling a bit.

"I wish it were, Rick. I wish it were. Follow me," said Stan.

Rick looked over his shoulder at Rita. She had already turned down Angle Avenue and was making her way back to the office. He heaved a sigh and followed Stan in the opposite direction.

◄○►

Stan and Rick walked past the building site where the mob of angry citizens was still gathered. The two of them took a shortcut through the dilapidated playground where Rick used to hang out as a kid. Crossing the street, they made their way past the courthouse, then the train station. Rick followed Stan around the back of the station to a small hidden stairway. Surprisingly, this whole area of Brickport was mostly still intact. It wasn't pretty, but it was holding together at least.

They walked through a narrow corridor to an unmarked door. Stan pushed the door open and gestured Rick inside. It was a bathroom. The entire thing was made of industrial gray bricks. The fixtures were made of black bricks.

"What are we doing here, Stan?" Rick asked. "Do you need to make a pit stop?"

"Well, yes, but that's not the whole reason we're here. We can kill two birds with one stone," Stan said.

Rick was starting to question his friend's judgment. He had known Stan quite a while, but not all that well. He was just a guy on the street whom he shared a coffee with a few times a week. And now Rick was following Stan into a strange, hidden bathroom to talk about the end of the world. It was nuts.

"Now," Stan said, lowering the cover to the toilet. "Stand up here and put your ear to the duct. Tell me what you hear."

"Stan, really . . ." Rick protested.

"Please, Rick. I promise it will all make sense soon."

Rick did as Stan asked. He stepped up onto the toilet seat and listened through the air duct. He heard voices. One of them sounded unmistakably like . . .

"Dr. Dubloon!" Rick gasped.

"Yes, Rick."

Dubloon was talking with someone who sounded like the mayor.

"You know, I'm taking a lot of heat for this project, Dubloon," said the mayor.

"Yes, yes, I'm sure it's very hard. You have my thanks," said Dr. Dubloon.

"The party wants to know why the unemployment rate is still so high, even with this huge construction project. Where are the jobs I promised? Where is the sense of community? I just want to make sure my voters . . ."

"I hired your beloved community member, Rick Brick, as promised. And the residents will love the final product. Fear not," said Dr. Dubloon.

"I just hope the payday is as big as you say it will be. I'm really sticking my neck out for this project," the major continued.

"Leave it to me, Minn," Dr. Dubloon said.

"I really prefer Ms. Mayor—"

"And I prefer Your Majesty, but we can't always have what we want, now, can we?" Dr. Dubloon joked.

"Ha, ha. Who knew that a sense of humor lurked under such a stern exterior?" said the mayor.

"It hides a great many things, Minn."

"What's so special about that brick you are saving for the opening ceremony, anyway?" asked the mayor. "Why is it so important?"

"Oh, it's significant to me, mostly. It has sentimental value. I don't know if others would find the same charms in it. Would you like to see it?"

"Of course."

Rick didn't like the way Dr. Dubloon's voice sounded. He never had a warm voice, but this cold, flat tone reminded Rick of the last time he'd spoken with the billionaire. It was enough to give a plastic man goose bumps.

There was a bit of a pause and the mayor spoke again.

"Why, it is rather . . . black," she said. Her voice sounded a little shaky all of a sudden. "It's really quite, um . . . oh no! What's happening to me? ACK!" she droned, in a tone that sounded startlingly familiar.

"Now, *Ms.* Mayor, about those voters . . . ," said Dr. Dubloon.

"Ack!"

"Yes, quite. Do you perceive this being a problem in the next election?"

"Ack!"

"Mmmm-hmmmm. Interesting. Well, I will miss our conversations, *Ms.* Mayor, but I'm glad we can work together on this. Heh. Heh. Heh Heh Heh," Dr. Dubloon cackled.

Rick slid back down to the floor. He could not believe what he'd just heard.

"My brother has been practicing that evil laugh since we were kids," said Stan. "He still hasn't nailed it."

"What are you saying, Stan?" Rick said.

"Well, he gets a bit self-conscious and it just doesn't have the right—"

"No! Not the laugh," said Rick. "Dr. Dubloon is your *brother*? What's he done to the mayor?"

"I can make a guess, my friend," said Stan. Rick didn't like the look on Stan's face. His friend sighed deeply and sat on the floor next to Rick.

"The mayor sounds just like Dr. Dubloon's crew at the worksite," said Rick. "Each has his own special grunt."

"It's happening, I'm afraid, Rick."

"What is?"

"The turning of the city," said Stan. "You wanted Brickport to be reborn—and after this project is complete it will be, but not in the way we always talked about. My dear brother, Dr. Dubloon, just turned the mayor into a grunt."

"A grunt?" said Rick thoughtfully.

"Yes, a grunt. A person who has lost her will. A puppet. A toy."

"But, how?" Rick asked, stunned.

Stan told Rick his story. The Dubloon brothers had grown up just after the Depression. Their father made his money in architecture and building, and was the first man to develop the locking brick. Before that, all the buildings had to be built again every three days. A good strong wind would knock a skyscraper flat! Both Stan and Francis, or Dr. Dubloon as he was now known, were raised to work in the family business. They had always fought quite a bit, but things got worse when Francis found out about the Onyx Brick.

"The Onyx Brick gives the bearer ultimate power," said Stan. "A man can use it to make anyone do his bidding. By forcing someone to look at it, the holder of the brick can change him from a normal, happy little figure with free will into one of those puppets—or grunts. People become mindless followers. He can get them to do anything he wants them to. I was afraid that had happened to you."

Rick glared at Stan. "It was our first job in a year. I had to take it! But if he's such a good architect, why does Dr. Dubloon need me?"

"Francis has made money in some . . . unusual ways in the past. He can't get the approvals he needs to build," said Stan. "And you may have noticed he's not very fun to work with. He's always alienating the community. Even *with* you and Rita running the site, the citizens of Brickport are turning against the project." Stan shook his head sadly. "If Francis creates a seat for the Onyx Brick—a niche that it fits in perfectly—the whole city and eventually the world will be his play set. He will control it all. That way he won't need to work with anyone. There might as well be only one person in the world if that happens—and that person will be Francis."

"That's why he wants to place the last brick himself," said Rick.

"Exactly."

"We have to stop him."

"I'm glad you agree."

"But how?"

‹○›

Rick and Stan agreed to meet the next morning disguised as two of Dr. Dubloon's grunts. Their plan was to sneak into Dr. Dubloon's headquarters and find the Onyx Brick. It was Saturday, so no one would be at the worksite except the protestors and the billionaire's cleanup crew.

On Saturday morning, Rick and Stan dressed in black coveralls and changed their heads to gray ones. After winding through the protestors, they entered the worksite. It was easy enough to blend in with the cleanup crew. Then Stan and Rick waited for the perfect moment to jump in a van that was bound for Dubloon's headquarters. It felt like hours passed before the van arrived, but once it did, Rick and Stan ducked in the back and waited.

The grunts carried materials to and from the van, but no driver came. Rick thought the sun would set and they would miss their chance. Then Dr. Dubloon showed up.

"You there!" he called to a grunt.

"Oof."

"I need you to take this back to headquarters," he commanded.

"Oof."

"It needs to go directly to mini grunt 52b, do you understand?"

"Oof."

The driver took the envelope from Dr. Dubloon and climbed into the driver's seat. Dr. Dubloon started to walk away. Stan and Rick ducked down to stay clear of the rearview mirror. They hid behind some boxes.

"On second thought," said Dr. Dubloon, walking toward the passenger side. "Maybe I better go with you."

Dr. Dubloon got in the van. Rick looked at Stan, who shrugged and motioned for Rick to keep quiet. Dr. Dubloon pulled hard on the van door in an effort to slam it closed, but it just came to a gentle rest, slightly open. He sighed and pulled on it firmly. The door latched with a gentle click. The grunt started the engine and drove. Rick stayed low behind a pile of boxes, trying to keep hidden from Dr. Dubloon. He peeked out the rear window to see where they were going. The van wound bumpily over the studded and broken streets behind the Dubloon Tower site and headed into an area of Brickport with ugly, beige warehouses. Tiles had fallen off here and there, and, like everywhere else, plates were missing from the road.

The van pulled into an underground garage. Nestled among the warehouses was Dubloon's headquarters.

"Okay, I'll take this up. You wait here," Dr. Dubloon ordered the grunt.

"Oof," said the grunt.

Rick and Stan stayed hidden in the back of the van until Dubloon disappeared up a stairwell. Then they carefully opened the van's back doors.

"OOF!" shouted the grunt from the front seat.

Rick and Stan made a run for it and dove into the stairwell. Dr. Dubloon was two flights up.

"Hey! I thought I told you to wait!" Dr. Dubloon called. He started back down the stairs. Stan gestured for Rick to follow him. They snuck down a flight of stairs and tucked themselves into a corner.

"Hello?" called Dr. Dubloon. "Where did that grunt go? Ah, well."

He climbed the stairs again. Rick and Stan waited. After about half an hour, Dr. Dubloon made his way down the stairs again. Rick and Stan waited until they heard the van's engine start, rev, and then grow distant.

"Where is Dubloon's office?" Rick asked.

"Shhh!" said Stan. "Keep your voice down." He beckoned Rick to follow.

At the top of the stairs were two security guard grunts. They were dressed in blue uniforms but had the gray faces of the Dubloon Tower workforce and a similar expression—or lack of expression. While Rick had never had any reason to suspect that the grunts at the site had any thought or feeling, these grunts seemed almost suspicious.

"GAH!" said the guard, menacingly. He reached for the Taser on his belt. Rick was about to run for it, but Stan restrained him.

"BAH!" said Stan to the guard. The guard looked confused.

"You speak Grunt?"

"It's easier than French," Stan said.

"GAH!" said the guard again and came after them. Stan swung at the guard's head and knocked it off.

"Holy cow! Stan!" said Rick.

"What? It's not like it won't go right back on," Stan said.

While the guard fumbled around for his head, Stan and Rick made their way up a second staircase.

When they reached the top, Stan put an ear to the door. He pulled a toolkit from the inside pocket of his trench coat and took a small screwdriver from it. Then he used it to fiddle with a metallic-looking plate at the door handle. After a few minutes, he dropped the screwdriver and punched the plate. It popped off, exposing some wires. He touched a red and a blue wire together, creating a small shower of sparks.

"Oooo," said Rick, impressed.

But the door remained closed. Stan kicked it, and it swung open. Once they were inside the room, Stan put the plate back in place and pulled the door closed so that it appeared to be latched.

"Francis thinks I'm no threat. But I always kept tabs on his security system," said Stan. "Remember, if we find the brick, don't look at it too closely."

Rick swallowed hard. He really had no idea what he was getting into.

There were no windows in the office—just walls of black bricks and a periscope pointing up from the desk. Opposite the desk was a wall full of shelves constructed from two-by-four black bricks. The top shelf held three large monitors. Stan hit the button on the center screen. Rick thought he might see a security camera view of the warehouse with a bunch of grunts moving things, or maybe the building site with a bunch of grunts moving things, or Dr.

Dubloon's living room with a bunch of grunts moving things. Instead, he saw a blockheaded cartoon character knocking another one over the head.

"Francis never could get enough of this show," Stan scoffed. He flicked it off in disgust. "We could never watch what I wanted to; it was always these stupid cartoon cavemen."

Down on the bottom shelf was a shiny flat door with a big dial in the center. Rick thought it must be a safe.

"Stan, look!" said Rick. He nodded at the safe.

"It's not in there."

"How do you know?"

"Because he's not just going to keep it in a safe. That's too obvious," Stan sighed.

"Then why are we here?" asked Rick.

"We're looking for clues," said Stan. Rick stared at him.

"Fine," said Stan. "You want me to look in the safe?"

Stan knelt down and put his ear to the safe door. He turned the dial back and forth a few times. Then he gave it a tug. The safe remained closed.

"It's probably just fake. To throw people like us off the trail." Stan sat down and leaned back on the fake safe. It popped open suddenly and Stan disappeared.

"Whoa!" yelled Stan.

"STAN!" Rick looked around. Then he peered through the safe door. He couldn't see anything but darkness. He thought about just closing the safe and sneaking back out of the office. Then he heard a clicking at the office door.

"Oooooog! Ooog!" It was a grunt, and he would be inside within seconds. Rick looked through the safe door again. Then he looked back at the office door. The guard from earlier stumbled in, struggling to reattach his head.

Rick sighed. "Well, here goes nothing."

He stuck his feet through the hole and pulled the door closed behind him. It was pitch black.

Then the floor dropped out from under him.

CHAPTER FOUR
THE GATE TO GOLD

Rick landed with a thud on a stack of toilet paper. He opened a door and emerged into the same bathroom he'd been in with Stan the other night.

"Oh, for Pete's sake, Stan."

"This is interesting," said Stan.

"Is it really? Because I'm beginning to feel like I'm chasing a wild goose. Only I have a feeling those Canada Geese by the port are much easier to catch than that mysterious Onyx Brick of yours," said Rick.

"Well, as I suspected, the safe does not hold the Onyx Brick," Stan said.

"Great. That's real progress. So now we have to figure out where it is, I suppose. Is this thing even for real? Or is it all some dark fantasy of yours?"

"Oh, it is quite real, indeed. Quite real. As real as the Gold Brick," Stan said, as he stroked his chin.

"I am really beginning to doubt my sanity," Rick said, then paused. "Wait. What? What do you mean, the Gold Brick? We're looking for the Onyx Brick."

"Or the Gold Brick," said Stan. "You see, if we get the Gold Brick, we may be able to block the effects of the Onyx Brick by the time my brother has a chance to lay it in the tower."

"And do we have any idea where this Gold Brick may be?" Rick asked.

"Oh, it's probably through the portal."

"The portal. I see. And where is the portal?"

Stan looked at the toilet. It was filled with little blue studs. Thankfully, that was all.

"Oh, for crying out loud, Stan! The portal's in a toilet?"

"Well, it's actually a fluid-based centrifugal time oscillator," Stan said matter-of-factly.

"That's it!" said Rick. "I have a job to do. It might not be the job I hoped for, but I committed to it. And I'm going to finish it, as promised."

"Rick, I know this is difficult to swallow. I do. But every word I've said is true. There is a Gold Brick and an Onyx Brick. And our beloved city is in danger. Now, if you need to take a little time to let that sink in, why, go right ahead. Take the rest of the weekend. But remember that the opening ceremony is approaching. You can find me at the coffee shop all day Monday if you change your mind."

"Yeah, well, I'm sorry, Stan. But you're going to be waiting a long time," said Rick as he marched out of the bathroom and toward home.

—◦—

Rick returned to the building site as planned on Monday morning. The protestors were thicker than ever before. They were packed shoulder-to-shoulder carrying signs. The phrases on their signs, however, no longer expressed concerns about the economy and jobs. They had taken a much darker turn: WHAT HAPPENED TO MY SON? ASK DR. DUBLOON; WHAT HAPPENED TO MY SISTER? ASK DR. DUBLOON; and one read, WHAT HAPPENED TO THE MAYOR?

The milling bodies that surrounded the barricades made it just about impossible to get into the site. Rick fought his way through for a good twenty minutes before Dr. Dubloon emerged. The billionaire threw a fistful of golden coins toward the back of the crowd. Surprisingly, it did little good. But Dr. Dubloon had his grunts carry him the rest of the way to the site's entrance. Rick didn't have the stomach to follow him. A man and his children stood steadfastly in front of Rick, blocking his path.

"We thought you were one of us, Rick Brick. You're just a pawn for that Dubloon fellow," said the man.

Rick felt terrible. Then Rita emerged from behind the barrier. She patted the man on the shoulder.

"Please, sir. I know this is difficult," said Rita.

"Where's my wife?" asked the man.

"I don't know, but we can't help find her unless you let us inside," said Rita. The man reluctantly moved aside. Rita and Rick made their way through a small door in the barrier.

"The mob has multiplied!" said Rick.

"I know. And they aren't just concerned about the lack of jobs anymore, Rick."

"Yes. I can see that." He thought about what he'd witnessed with Stan on Saturday, and suddenly the dark fantasy seemed very real. What else could be responsible for the shells of people he saw walking around the worksite? There seemed to be more of them, too. Something was very wrong, and Rick couldn't ignore it any more.

Rick and Rita made their way toward the entrance of the nearly finished tower. Black bricks were stacked up together to create glossy, smooth walls as far as the eye could see. Everything, including staircases and the elevators, was built with black or industrial gray. The building was solid and serious. There weren't any flourishes but one. Right near the entrance was an area surrounded by a thick plastic bubble—a kind of clear vault. Rick had never seen anything like it. In the center of the bubble was an oddly notched space. It was a space that would be filled by one brick and one brick only. That was the Onyx Brick, Rick realized. And that brick had a frightening job. It seemed to be the only space that mattered to Dubloon and he was already there, standing over it.

"Good morning, Brick. Rita," the doctor said.

Dr. Dubloon took pictures of the niche and measured it, then paced back and forth rubbing his chin. He took out a white handkerchief and buffed the bubble. Some of the grunts started to mimic him. Every now and then he would rub his little hooked hands together and chuckle, "Heh Heh Heh," and the grunts would echo him. Stan was right. Dr. Dubloon had a pathetic evil laugh.

"We need to act, Rick," said Rita quietly. "There's something very wrong with this project."

"Agreed," said Rick.

Perhaps he didn't need to travel through some mystical septic system to save the world. Perhaps he could just confront Dr. Dubloon right now. Rick approached his client.

"Dr. Dubloon?"

"Ah, Brick. The tower is spectacular. We are nearly ready for the ceremony. It's exciting, isn't it? Can you feel that energy in the air?"

"Well, there is a lot of energy. But is it the kind of energy we want? I mean, the protestors . . ."

"Forget the protestors!" Dr. Dubloon yelled. Rick thought he saw the man's eyes turn red. Then the doctor grew suddenly calm again. "It's just the storm before the calm, Brick."

"I think it's usually the other way around, Sir," Rick said.

"Not in this case. I have a plan," said Dr. Dubloon.

"What kind of plan?" Rick asked.

"You know," Dr. Dubloon said, placing his arm stiffly over Rick's shoulders. "I just had this conversation with the mayor, in fact . . ."

"Oh, good!" said Rick. "I guess you two have got it covered, then! I'm going to find Rita. There's still so much to be done!"

Rick knew he had to go see Stan, and fast. He gathered his coat and his canvas workbag and made his way to see Rita.

"Rita. I've got something I have to do," said Rick.

"Is there any way I can help?" Rita asked.

"I have a plan. Let's talk when I get back," said Rick. As he opened the door to the barrier he looked back. Rita was standing there staring at him. She seemed worried.

◄○►

Rick couldn't find Stan at the coffee shop at first, so he waited. The place was nearly empty. The few people there lifted their cups awkwardly from the studs on the tables and brought them to their mouths. Rick waited and waited. After about twenty minutes, Rita showed up.

"Rita!" said Rick. "What are you doing here?"

"I was worried." Rita said with a shrug. "And if you've got a plan, I want in."

"It's a long story. And you may not be so enthusiastic when you hear what the plan is," said Rick.

Rick told Rita about the Gold and Onyx Bricks, about the portal, and about Stan and Dr. Dubloon. She looked at him very skeptically.

"I know it may seem like it," said Rick, "but I really haven't lost my mind."

"Well, we've been partners for ten years," said Rita, "and we've been through a lot together. I guess I can follow you through this crazy portal—if it even exists."

"You should probably see the portal before you decide," said Rick.

Rick was about to explain when Stan showed up.

"It's been almost two hours!" said Rick. "I thought you said you'd be here!"

"I thought you said I'd be waiting a while," said Stan. "I'm glad you bought a friend. Hello, Rita. It's good to see you."

"Hello, Stan," said Rita.

"I've never been down a toilet before," said Rick. "I wasn't sure what to wear for the occasion."

"Wait a minute . . . down a toilet?" asked Rita.

"Listen, can we just get this trip over with?" said Rick. "Are you still in, Rita?"

Rita sighed. "Let's see the toilet first."

‹◦›

Rick and Rita followed Stan through the winding path to the secret door. They tried to open it, but it wouldn't budge. Stan reached his curved hands around the edge of the door and gave it a tug. Still no luck. Finally, he pounded on the door with his little hooked fists. He was about to remove it from its plastic hinges.

A voice from inside called, "Do you mind?"

"Who's that?" asked Rick.

"How am I supposed to know?" Stan responded.

They heard the toilet flush. Then it flushed again. Stan looked at Rick. Rick looked at Rita. The door opened. A man in a Parks Service uniform walked out.

"Geez. Give a guy a break." The man walked away muttering.

Once he was out of sight, Rick, Rita, and Stan checked to see if anyone was watching, then they all stepped inside the bathroom. It was very close quarters.

"So, how does this thing work?" asked Rick.

"Hold on just a second, and I'll show you," said Stan. "Patience, my boy."

Stan hooked the edge of a trapdoor in the floor with his hands and pulled it open.

"Oh, wow! That's funny," said Rita, breathing a sigh of relief. "You know, I thought that the portal was going to actually be in the toilet."

"Oh, this isn't the portal. I'm just adjusting the water flow," Stan said.

"Oh," Rita said, disappointed.

"Hop in, Rick," said Stan.

Rick looked inside the black toilet bowl. "Ladies first?" he said to Rita with a timid gesture.

"I don't think so, Boss," said Rita.

"Oh, so I'm the boss when it comes to being flushed down a toilet, huh?" Rick said. "Why don't you go first, Stan? You know the way."

"Do you know how to operate the fluid-based time oscillator, Rick?" asked Stan.

"I'd like to think so," said Rick.

"Well, I'm not going anyway," said Stan.

"What?" Rick and Rita said, almost at the same time.

"Someone has to hold down the fort here," said Stan. "Besides, I get awful motion sickness. Just follow my instructions and you should be okay." He handed Rick a hefty instruction book.

"Fine," said Rick. He and Rita reviewed the book quickly.

"We won't get stuck in another time period, will we?" asked Rita.

"Hold onto the instructions and you should be okay. They can help you out of any situation," said Stan. "Now, Rick . . ." He gestured toward the toilet.

Rick removed a spray bottle of disinfectant from the supply closet. He gave the bowl a thorough spritz.

"I assure you that's not necessary," said Stan.

"Says the man who's staying behind," Rick grumbled. He gingerly stepped into the toilet and held his nose. Stan put his hand on the flusher and gave it a firm push. He held it down and counted, "One, two, three . . ."

Rick didn't hear the rest. It was muffled by the clatter of blue and clear studs in the bowl. He felt a strong pulling sensation and heard Rita's voice in the distance.

"See you soon!" she called.

Rick wondered if he really would.

CHAPTER FIVE
DOWN THE TOILET

R ick felt as though he were caught inside a Chinese finger trap. After what seemed like hours, he landed with a heavy thud beneath a circle of large, strange-looking trees. All around him were big, shiny leaves like giant, green hands—large enough to use as blankets—and big, thick blades of grass. The vegetation was so dense that he couldn't see the baseplate it was affixed to. Rick stood up a bit too quickly and felt dizzy. He dropped to his knees again and lowered his head to his hands, trying to steady himself. When he lifted his face again, Rick found himself looking into a big eye on a shiny green head. The eye seemed to take up most of the head. If he hadn't known better, he'd have thought it belonged to a dinosaur.

"Ahhhhhhhh!" Rick screamed.

The startled green head popped up and away from Rick. It sat on top of a long neck that was attached to a gigantic body by a hinge.

Then Rita landed beside him with a thud. Rick was relieved to see his friend's face.

"Glad you could make it," he said.

"Blech," she replied. "I'd rather not repeat that journey, thank you very much."

The huge head sank down again and sniffed at Rita warily. Then it rubbed gently against Rick's back.

"Who's your friend?" asked Rita.

Rick ignored her question. "Where are we?" he wondered aloud.

"Well, judging from your buddy the Brachiosaurus," said Rita, "we're in the Jurassic period."

"And where is the Gold Brick?" asked Rick.

Rita removed the sack from her shoulder and pulled out Stan's instructions.

"It should be somewhere under this tree," said Rita. "We just need to look around for it."

Rita and Rick moved some of the larger leaves aside. They picked up a big, gray, rock-shaped block. It took both of them to move it. Alas, there was no brick underneath. They moved more baseplates. Rita climbed the tree and shook the branches. A coconut fell out and hit Rick on the head.

"Ow!" he cried.

"Oops. Sorry about that," said Rita. "I guess it's not up here, either." She shinnied back down.

Rick sighed. He tried to rest his face in his hands and nearly poked himself in the eye. A hot, gusty breath blasted his ear. The big herbivore was sniffing at him again.

"Hey, cut that out!" said Rick. "It tickles."

"Looks like this Brachiosaurus has taken a liking to you, Rick," said Rita.

Rick looked into the big eye of the Brachiosaurus again.

"He reminds me of the dog I had when I was a kid. His name was Sparkles," said Rick. "He ran away when I was about ten."

"MEEERRRRGGHHH," said the creature.

"I think I'll call him Sparkles II," said Rick.

"Mmmmm. Original," said Rita. Rick shot Rita a dirty look.

"Hey, wait a second," said Rita. "What's that on his back?"

Sure enough, a shiny gold brick was stuck to the big dinosaur's back. It had an irregular shape and glinted tauntingly in the sunlight.

"I knew there was a reason I liked you," said Rick.

Just then, a not-so-friendly sound emerged from around the edge of a large fern.

"EEEEEEEERRRRRRR. EEEEERRRRR!"

"Don't look now," said Rick, "but here comes Sparkle II's mom."

"Uh-oh."

But instead of running toward his mother's call, Sparkles II bounded into the jungle. He seemed to think it was all a big game. Rick and Rita ran to try to catch up, but it was no use. The dinosaur was too big and fast. Then, just when they thought they had lost him, Sparkles II turned around and galloped back toward them, like a dog playing keep-away with a ball. Unfortunately, the ball was a brick that was crucial to the safety of Brickport and the world!

After about an hour of playing keep-away, Rick and Rita decided to try another plan. They hid so the dinosaur would stop and wait for them, thinking they were farther down the path. Rick climbed a tree and covered himself in its leaves. Rita crouched in the dense brush on the ground. Sure enough, Sparkles II loped back toward them and stopped, right below Rick's tree, just as they had hoped he would.

"Meeerrrrghhh?"

Rick dropped down, right on top of Sparkles II and the brick.

"Gotcha!" Rick cried.

Instantly, Sparkles II took off at full speed. He didn't even seem to feel Rick on his back. He was still playing. He jumped over clusters of ferns and small bushes—even a medium-sized tree. Rick was like a little flag waving from atop the Brachiosaurus's back. Finally, Rick shifted back just enough to dislodge the Gold Brick. He fell hard . . . into a big pool of mud.

Rita ran up and knelt beside him.

"Oh my, Rick, are you o . . ." She sniffed. "Ugh."

Rick had not landed in mud after all.

"Aw, man," said Rick, getting a whiff of himself.

"At least the poop cushioned your fall," said Rita. "And you got the Gold Brick!"

"Now we can go home!" said Rick.

"Yes!" said Rita. "We just have to figure out these instructions from Stan for building a portal."

They looked at Stan's instructions. It was going to take a while.

—◄o►—

After spending most of the afternoon and early evening trying to make sense of the directions in

Stan's book, Rick and Rita decided to find a safe place to sleep and try again in the morning. Rick found a creek nearby to wash the stink off, and they made a bed with some bundles of leaves they'd collected and went to sleep.

Rick woke in the early dawn and got Rita up. They started working right away, and the instructions made a little more sense since they had a good night's sleep. Rita had some bricks in the work sack she'd brought with her, and Rick had managed to scavenge some other pieces from the jungle set they'd landed in. By the time the sun was up over the shiny green foliage, they nearly had the portal finished. There were just a couple of spots that they could not find the right bricks for. But Rita came up with an alternate plan.

"I think I've just about got it, Rick," said Rita. She leaned into a corner piece trying to get it to snap in place.

"Great," replied Rick, with as much energy as he could muster. He added his weight to Rita's effort, and the pieces snapped together. He was excited to be going home, but he was also tired. The day before had been full of strange surprises, lots of work, and dinosaur rustling. After his fall, his arms seemed to pop off a little too easily. He looked up from their portal, and he could see Sparkles II lurking behind a tree. The dinosaur had the same eager expression that he'd had the day before.

"What are you looking at, Buddy?" asked Rick. "We've got no time to play today."

It was true that Sparkles II was a pest, but Rick couldn't help feeling warm toward the big creature. After all, Sparkles II had no idea he was making Rick's life more difficult; he just wanted to play!

"That should do it!" said Rita.

"You found something for H5, too?" asked Rick, looking over Rita's shoulder at the instructions.

"Yeah, I think these two-by-twos snapped together will do the job," said Rita. "A job for every brick and each brick in its place."

"Hey, that's what I always say," said Rick. Rita smiled.

"Well, there's a little more air between them than I would like," said Rita.

"Yeah, but I don't see how we have much choice," said Rick. The pieces they'd stuck together weren't really meant to lock in place, but with a little force they had managed to jam them into one another pretty snugly.

While they were looking over their work, Sparkles II snuck up behind them. The Gold Brick was just inside the sack at Rita's feet. Before Rick and Rita had even noticed the big beast, he grabbed the brick and bounded back behind the tree.

"Oh no, Sparkles II!" cried Rick. "Please! Not today." Rick seemed to be torn between chasing after the naughty dino and calling it quits. He knew he couldn't leave without the Gold Brick, though. He decided to try to outwit Sparkles II. He picked up a big stick and waved it in the air.

"C'mon Sparkles II! C'mon!" said Rick.

Sparkles II wagged his big tail clumsily, taking out a couple of trees behind him.

Rick threw the stick. Unfortunately, it went right through the portal, along with his arm. Sparkles II followed right behind them. He still had the brick in his mouth.

CHAPTER SIX
DINOSAUR IN SPACE

Rick had thought that the sucking feeling he'd experienced from the first portal journey had been due to the flush. But, as it turned out, that pull was just the sensation of passing from one time period to another. This time, as he launched through the portal, he felt as though he were being squeezed through a tube of toothpaste. Rick saw the gray ground below him, but he couldn't reach it. He was floating just above it. He looked around and realized he was surrounded by clusters of light—stars.

For a moment, Rick was really excited. As a boy, he had always dreamed of traveling to the moon. But the excitement soon gave way to fear. Where was Rita? How would they get home again? What about the Gold Brick? What about his arm? Luckily, Rick didn't need a space helmet. He had no lungs. Still, he missed the feeling of good, solid walls around him and the ground beneath his feet.

Just below Rick was a space station. By waving his remaining arm back and forth furiously, he was able to move down just an inch or so— far enough to attach his foot to the station's roof. Then he pulled himself inside through a hatch in the top. He closed the hatch tightly and dropped to the floor.

"Ah, gravity, old friend!" Rick took two steps forward and stepped on an old banana peel. His feet shot out from under him. He landed hard on his butt.

"Good thing no one was here to see that," Rick said to himself. He looked up through the window. To his surprise, there was Rita looking in. He couldn't hear her laugh, but he saw her shoulders shaking. He had a good mind to lock the hatch and leave her out there. Then she waved at him . . . using *his* arm.

He climbed up a ladder to the overhead hatch and opened it. Rita dropped inside. She tried to suppress her giggle. Rick took his arm from her and popped it back on.

"Thanks," said Rick. "Have you seen Sparkles II or the Gold Brick out there?"

"Yeah, that crazy dinosaur keeps floating by, but I can't get hold of him," said Rita. "It's going to take two of us."

They found some spacesuits in a hatch inside the space station. Luckily, they were equipped with intercoms and boots that would help them stick to the moon's baseplates. Rick and Rita put them on. They scavenged some other materials—bricks, propellers, wheels, and other pieces—just in case. Then they headed outside to find Sparkles II and the Gold Brick.

Now that Rick knew his friend was safe nearby, he could enjoy the view a bit more. He guessed that they were, indeed, on the moon, because he could see the curve of Earth just over the horizon. It was a magnificent swirl of blue and white. As the pair moved closer to the horizon, they could see even more of Earth. Then their favorite dinosaur appeared.

Rick called out and pointed. "Sparkles II!"

"Yep. I see him, Rick."

Rita and Rick stopped and waited for Sparkles II to float closer. Rick hoisted Rita onto his shoulders, and just as Sparkles II's rear leg was about to float by, she snagged it and attached it to the top of her helmet. Rick helped her down to the moon's surface and then stuck her boots to the baseplates so she wouldn't float away.

"Look at me! I can balance a dinosaur on my head!" Rita called out.

"All right, Rita," said Rick. "Quit joking around."

"It's better than your banana peel trick," said Rita.

Rick gave her a dirty look. "Can you get out the instruction book, please, so we can get home?"

Rita sighed. She pulled out the book and turned it to the portal-building page. Before they started building, they tethered Sparkles II to the ground and made sure the Gold Brick was still attached to him. It was! Then they got to work. The building went faster this time because they were familiar with the process. When they got to the last few steps, they had to get a little creative with their use of bricks again. Rick studied the instructions in the book so he would have a good idea of what bricks might serve their purpose. He set the book down and fished through Rita's bag for bricks. Rita was checking over their work.

"Rick, have you seen the instructions?" asked Rita.

Rick looked at Rita's sack where he had left the book. He untucked the sack from where it was anchored beneath the space station and looked inside. But there was no book to be found.

"Are you sure you don't have them?" asked Rick.

"No!" said Rita, alarmed. Then she looked overhead and saw that the book was floating away.

"Quick! Give me a leg up!" said Rita.

Rick hoisted Rita up, but the book was out of reach. It was floating gently away. Rick looked around for a stick or something he could reach the book with, but there was nothing. The instructions were lost.

"Great," said Rick.

CHAPTER SEVEN
BACK TO EARTH

Now what?" said Rick.

"Don't ask me. You're the one who lost the instructions," said Rita.

"I didn't lose them, I . . ." but Rick stopped himself. He realized he probably had lost the instructions after all.

"Okay, listen," he said to Rita. "I'm sure we can figure something out." He rummaged through Rita's bag again and found a propeller. He attached it to a belt and some pedals, and then he stuck it to his back. It was his own personal helicopter! He stuck his feet on the pedals and pumped furiously. Because there was no atmosphere on the moon, there was not much for the propeller to push against. Still, he rose enough to get closer to the book. With one final push he was within arm's length. He reached out and grabbed it by a page. The page tore. He pressed the pedals again and got a little closer. At last he grabbed it.

"Got it!" Rick said through the intercom.

"Great! Now, how are you going to get back?" asked Rita.

Rick looked down. The moon was much farther below than he realized. He wondered if he could simply turn upside down and pedal downward.

"Hold on. Sparkles II and I have it covered," said Rita.

She scaled the dinosaur and reached up. Her fingers just brushed Rick's boot—close but not close enough. Sparkle II didn't seem to like the fact that his friend was floating away, either. Pulling his front feet away from the baseplates, the dinosaur rose up on his hind legs. Rita climbed up to Sparkles II's head and grabbed Rick's leg.

Safely on the ground again, Rick stowed his makeshift helicopter in Rita's bag. He pulled out the two bricks he thought they could use to finish the portal, and then he opened the instruction book to the page with the portal instructions. As luck would have it, though, that was the page that had torn.

"Nice," said Rita.

"Hold on," said Rick. "We can do this. The portal is pretty much finished. We can use these two bricks for that final slot." He held up a piece that he had cobbled together. "It's pretty much the same as last time."

"But last time we ended up here! On the moon!" said Rita.

"Do you see a rocket or shuttle anywhere?" asked Rick. "This is our only way out of here. And we have a city to save." Rick hoped that sounded convincing, because he wasn't feeling so heroic at the moment.

"You're right, Rick," said Rita.

Rick, and Rita pressed the two bricks together as hard as they could. They gave the portal a final inspection.

"Ready?" asked Rita.

"Ladies first!" Rick said, enthusiastically.

Rita stepped through. Rick was about to follow her when he realized they were leaving something important behind. He walked over to Sparkles II and pulled the Gold Brick from the dinosaur's nose. He petted the beast and looked into his big eye.

"We don't have time to bring you back, Buddy," said Rick, "but someone is bound to come through here again. You'll make another friend soon. A better friend than I am." He turned away.

"Meerghh?" said Sparkles II sadly.

Slowly, Rick turned around.

—◁◦▷—

Moments later, Rick felt the familiar squeeze and he landed, hard, next to Rita. Then Sparkles II landed on top of him.

"Oof!" The baseplates below them threatened to crack.

"You brought Sparkles II?" said Rita.

"Well . . ." said Rick. He stuck the Gold Brick on Sparkles II's belly and pulled himself out from underneath him. Rick looked above him at a magnificent, sand-colored structure. It rose up to a point that seemed to disappear into the sky. They had landed in ancient Egypt.

"So much for getting home," Rick sighed.

"At least we get to see some really cool architecture," said Rita. "We better get to work, though. The Egyptians might not take kindly to a big monster and two people in weird clothes near their pyramids."

It was then that Rick realized he was still in his space suit—and it was hot! Both Rick and Rita pulled their jumpsuits off and looked around for more materials to start building their new portal. In the distance, a group of little figures carried a litter. Someone important-looking rode inside. They seemed to be moving closer.

"I hope we have time to finish," said Rita, as she busily snapped bricks together.

"Maybe they'll think we're gods?" said Rick.

"Or aliens!" said Rita.

They worked quickly and got to the same sticky spot that had given them trouble before.

"Let me just take a look around the pyramid and see if I can find something that will work," said Rita. She wandered around to the other side. Rick watched as Rita disappeared around the corner of the enormous structure. The bricks all fit smoothly together. One just seemed to gradually flow into the next and the whole thing sparkled in the sunlight. How wonderful it must have felt to make something like that!

Rick turned back to check on the progress of the litter. It was no longer so far away. He could see that a few people in the group had noticed them.

"Rita!" he called. "We better get moving."

"Okay," Rita called back. She dashed around to the front of the pyramid and dropped down beside Rick. She seemed a little nervous. "I . . . uh . . . think I found the perfect piece! What do you know?" She clicked it into place.

"Wow," said Rick. "That is perfect! Where did you find . . . uh-oh." There was a large rumbling sound behind them. It was coming from the pyramid.

"Rita?"

"Who would have thought that one brick held up the whole thing?" said Rita.

Three figures with long spears and golden headpieces broke away from the group guarding the litter and ran toward them, shouting. The language wasn't familiar, but Rick thought he understood the gist.

"MEERRRRGH!!" yelled Sparkles II in response.

"Should we try to fix it?" asked Rita.

"There's no time for that!" yelled Rick. Pieces of the pyramid were already starting to fall. The men were upon them with spears raised, but the dinosaur seemed to make them hesitate.

"C'mon, Sparkles II, let's go!" Rick gave his pet a shove through the portal and jumped through after him. Rita followed.

CHAPTER EIGHT
ALMOST HOME

Rick felt that familiar squeezing sensation and then landed on Sparkles II, who objected loudly.

"MEEERRGH!" The dinosaur's call was a bit muffled. His neck reached clear through the ceiling. Rick couldn't even see where his head was.

"Sorry, Buddy," said Rick.

"MEEERRGH!" Sparkles II repeated.

"Keep it down up there! You're going to get us in trouble," said Rick.

They were crammed into a closet. Rick caught a nauseating wave of air freshener, and his arm had popped off again, but at least he was back in Brickport.

"I never thought I'd be so happy to see a public restroom," he said to Sparkles II.

"Meeeerrgggh?"

A second later, Rita landed behind Rick and handed him his arm.

"Hey, thanks!" said Rick.

A piece of the ceiling fell. This was the last straw for the Brachiosaurus. He burst through the bathroom door with a bellow.

"MEEEERRRRGGGGGH!"

On the other side was a man with a familiar poof of red hair and serious eyebrows.

"Ah, Brick! You've arrived just in time to see me foil all your plans!" Dr. Dubloon said triumphantly. He held the Gold Brick aloft.

"The Gold Brick!" said Rick.

"Gold travels faster than plastic, Brick. I'm so sorry to see you waste all your time and energy, but I just couldn't stand the wretched colors you planned to bring to this city. Also, I don't like to share. Tootle-oo!" Dubloon burst out the door and onto the street.

Rick and Rita tried to give chase on Sparkles II, but they had to burst through all the bricks to get the beast onto the street. They arrived outside just in time to see Dr. Dubloon jump into a van and peel out.

"I want to cry," said Rick.

"I want to pull someone's arms off," said Rita.

Rick's arms fell off just then.

"Not yours," said Rita.

Before they even had a chance to decide what their next step was, Stan arrived.

"The heroes return!" said Stan. "Nice pet, by the way."

"Thanks," said Rick, glumly. Rick and Rita still hadn't moved from Sparkles II's back.

"Why the long faces?"

"Dr. Dubloon just made off with the Gold Brick," said Rita.

"Really? Well, what's that stuck to the dino's belly then?" Stan asked.

Rick slid down Sparkles II's neck and looked at his underside. Sure enough, there was the Gold Brick!

"Then what was . . .?"

"The old fake brick trick, Rick," said Stan. "I decided to leave it in the bathroom in case Francis came a-calling. And, sure enough . . ."

"Wow! That's fantastic," said Rita. "Thanks, Stan!"

"No, thank *you*!" said Stan. "Now we have to get back to our own time period."

"Wait," said Rick. "I thought we were back. When's this?"

"This is just about a year ahead of our time, Rick," said Stan. "My brother couldn't help himself. He had to see what would happen to Brickport. And then when he saw it, he had to destroy it, of course."

Suddenly Rick looked around and noticed all the bright new construction. It wasn't quite a new city yet, but it was on its way. "So, we won?" said Rick. "This is *our* Brickport? The one we dreamed of?"

"Well, almost. But we haven't 'won' quite yet. Francis still has the Onyx Brick. He can still do plenty of damage. We have to get back and stop him," said Stan. "But maybe you'd like to look around the place? For inspiration?"

"You know it!" said Rita.

"Okay, let's take a walk by the port. That's where all the good stuff is," said Stan.

"I always knew that was the best place to rebuild," said Rick.

They headed down the street toward the water. The change along the port was miraculous.

"Wow!" said Rita.

All the green spaces—the picnic areas, the baseball fields, the soccer fields—had had green baseplates added to fill in the broken spaces. There was also a big Ferris wheel, just like the one that Rick had always dreamed of having. It was as spectacular as the ones in other great cities like Paris and Sydney. But perhaps the best thing that Rick saw was a big mosaic just before the entrance to the Ferris wheel. It was a large, colorful frame that read BUILD A DREAM. Near it were piles of bricks that children were using to finish the picture.

"This is amazing," said Rick. He almost had to pinch himself. But just as he was about to drop to his knees to help the children build, he felt a gentle nudge on his shoulder.

"Meerrrggh?" Sparkles II sounded almost concerned.

"What is it, Buddy?"

Rick looked off past the Ferris wheel and the mosaic—down toward the other end of the port. The colorful oasis that he'd been lost in for the last few minutes gradually changed into a black, shiny industrial complex. And all around it were the grayish drones he recognized from Dubloon Tower.

"Rita," he said to his partner while he kept his eyes fixed on the grim horizon, "we better get back—and fast!"

CHAPTER NINE
A CITY OF GRUNTS

The group hurried back to the portal and transported to their own, present-day Brickport. There was still a lot to do and not much time to do it. While Rick and Rita had managed to get the Gold Brick, the Onyx Brick was still in the evil clutches of Dr. Dubloon, and the Grand Ceremony for the Dubloon Tower was only two days away. The friends would have to work fast to save Brickport from certain doom.

After popping out of the toilet, Rita, Rick, and Stan hopped aboard Sparkles II and headed to Starbricks to concoct a plan. But their old favorite coffee place was not what it once was. It wasn't empty, for one thing. Rather, it was filled with grunts. They were all holding Starbricks mugs and mimicking Dr. Dubloon's evil laugh: "HEH HEH. HEH HEH." They lifted their cups high, as if proposing a toast, and brought them clumsily to their mouths, which were always ajar. One of them missed his mouth entirely and went straight for the forehead. It was unsettling—all those gray-faced grunts milling around, laughing like buffoons. Rick couldn't understand it. Even if Dr. Dubloon did want to rule the world, why would he want these guys for company?

As if he heard Rick's thoughts, Stan spoke up. "Francis never did have many friends, Rick. Perhaps these grunts are better than no one."

"Barely," said Rick. "I'd prefer . . . I'd prefer . . ."

Just then Rick felt something nudge his shoulder.

"Meeeerrggghhhh," Sparkles II hummed contentedly.

"Awwwww," said Rita, and she gave him a pet on the head.

"AWWWWW. AWWWWW." Suddenly the grunts wandered over to the three of them. They all milled around Sparkles II.

"We better get out of here," said Rick. "These guys are really starting to give me the creeps."

The three friends wandered out of the coffee shop and toward Rita and Rick's office. Rita and Rick walked beside Sparkles II, to reassure him, while Stan rode on the dinosaur's back. Everywhere they looked they saw grunts. There were still regular folks, but the population of those transformed by Dr. Dubloon and the Onyx Brick had doubled.

"How are we going to get the Onyx Brick away from Dr. Dubloon?" asked Rita.

Sparkles II gently nudged Rita's hand. "Oh, you!" she said and pet him gently. He nuzzled her hand. "Awww," she said again.

"AWWWWW. AWWWWWW," said a bunch of grunts trailing behind them. "AWWWWWW."

Rick and Rita stopped walking and Sparkles II stopped beside them. The grunts stopped walking, too. Rick pet Sparkles II.

"They really seem to like Sparkles II," said Rick.

"AWWWWWW," said the grunts.

"Who can blame them?" said Rita.

"Wait a second!" said Rick. "That gives me an idea."

-◄◦►-

Stan agreed to meet Rick and Rita the next morning before the dedication ceremony. In the meantime, Rita and Rick went down to the port. They figured it would give them plenty of space to work on "Project

Sparkles II." They were also confident that they wouldn't run into Dr. Dubloon or his grunts there. Dr. Dubloon made his hatred for the harbor quite clear. Rita had also been stashing a bunch of old bricks from the tower building site down by the docks in the hopes they could use them for another project.

"Since Dr. Dubloon doesn't like colors, I didn't think he would miss these," Rita said, showing Rick the collection she had stowed in a cluster of bushes.

"You've been collecting these all this time?" said Rick.

"I figured we would need them eventually," said Rita, "and we do!"

Rick liked the idea that Rita was still thinking about other projects even as they were working on Dubloon Tower. It was nice to know his partner felt the way that he did about the city and still wanted to try to improve it for its citizens.

Rick and Rita sorted the pieces by color and then got to work. They replaced Sparkles II's solid belly with a hollow one. Then, they installed a trapdoor with a roll-out ladder. When the door was closed, it fit so neatly you couldn't tell it was there unless you were looking for it. Rita added some chairs and plastic brick grass inside so it would feel cozy. She also included a little scope in the chest, so Sparkles II's passengers could see what was going on. Rick put together a little refrigerator and a snack bar, just in case they got hungry.

Rick was eager to try out the new and improved Brachiosaurus. He scrambled up the ladder and sprawled out on the grass inside.

"Ahhh," he sighed. Then he called out to Rita, "Once we're done saving the city, maybe we can take Sparkles II camping!"

When they had completed their renovations, Sparkles II could seat four passengers comfortably, but he would only really need to hold three—Rick, Rita, and Stan. Since they were having fun building, they decided to make the outside of Sparkles II look more festive for the occasion—like a big, sparkly present for the city. They added little brick jewels, some brick flowers, and a big bow tie. He was still the same old endearing dinosaur, with some colorful enhancements.

"I always wanted a pony when I was growing up," said Rita, "but Sparkles II might be even better."

"Yeah, he's pretty special," said Rick, patting the Brachiosaurus's long neck. "Irresistible, you might say."

"Shall we take him for spin?" said Rita.

"MEEERRRRGGGHHH," said the new, improved Sparkles II.

"That sounds like a yes!" said Rick.

They thought it best if Rick guided Sparkles II while Rita rode, and then they could switch. They didn't want Sparkles II wandering willy-nilly all over the city. At first, he was uncomfortable with the little person in his belly, but once he realized it was just his friend Rita, he was quite happy to have her there. They walked back toward the office by the field near the band shell. Rick was excited to see more greenery here and lots of kids playing. The children started to notice Sparkles II and joined them on their stroll. Eventually, it seemed that Sparkles II had attracted every child in the park, and even some adults. They created an odd little parade of Brickportians. Despite his size, Sparkles II did not scare anyone. In fact, they all seemed to love him!

Finally, it was time to head home. Rick, Rita, and Sparkles II needed their rest. It had been a long day and they had to be fresh for the ceremony. They let some of the children take a ride inside Sparkles II before they headed away from the water and waved goodbye. Rick climbed up the ladder and inside Sparkles II, and Rita walked beside the dinosaur as they made their way into town.

"It's pretty cozy up here," said Rick.

When they turned from the port, it immediately felt a little colder and bleaker to Rick.

"MEEERGH-CHOO," Sparkles II sneezed. Rick fell backwards, right through the trapdoor and onto the rough sidewalk.

"Ouch!"

"Are you okay?" asked Rita.

"Yeah, I think so," said Rick. "But could you help me get my arm back on?"

"Awww, poor Rick," said Rita.

"AWWWWW," a lone grunt echoed. He had already noticed their charismatic pet.

"Uh-oh, we better get out of here," said Rita. She and Rick snapped his arm back on and they high-tailed it toward home.

Despite not liking the grunt, at least Rick and Rita knew that the new Sparkles II was still attractive to the gray people. It looked like their plan was going to work!

―◦―

Rick and Rita had planned to meet Stan at eight in the morning at the corner near Starbricks—two hours before the ceremony was scheduled to begin. They were to bring Sparkles II as close as they could to the tower and then make their way inside, using the dinosaur as both a distraction and a vehicle. The grunts were so captivated by him that they would just let him straight inside—at least that's what they hoped! Rita gave Rick her bag with some spare parts, just in case. Most importantly, they had painted the Gold Brick black to resemble the Onyx Brick.

Rick climbed up and settled himself and his tools inside their plush new dino-den.

But they had run into a little problem. It seemed that Sparkles II wasn't adjusting well to the change in climate. He kept having sneezing fits, and Rick was regularly being dumped onto the street through the trapdoor.

"Why do we have such a lousy door?" asked Rick. "Surely there's got to be a better way to keep something closed than this little plastic thing."

"Maybe we should turn the door around. You know, so it opens inward," said Rita.

"Nah, then it's more visible. Let's just put this brick over the opening," said Rick.

"Suit yourself," said Rita. "I don't know, though. Seems a little awkward."

"Ah, it'll be fine," said Rick.

They made their way to the corner by the coffee shop and waited. Soon Rick could hear Stan talking to Rita and Sparkles II outside.

"Hey Sparkles II, ol' pal," said Stan. "You're looking pretty sharp, Buddy."

"MEEERRRRGGGHHH-CHOOOO!" The door popped open and Rick fell right on top of Stan.

"Well, good morning to you, too," said Stan, standing and dusting himself off.

Stan followed Rick up the ladder and back inside Sparkles II's belly. He looked around and gave an impressed whistle.

"I love what you've done with the . . . uh . . . pet," he said.

"Thanks, Stan," said Rick.

"I'll be down here with Sparkles II," called Rita. "Give a holler if you need anything."

Rick pulled the door closed and put the brick back over the opening.

"That could have used a little more thought," said Stan.

"It's fine," said Rick.

"Suit yourself," Stan replied.

Stan told Rita to follow Rotor Boulevard straight up toward Dubloon Tower. There were grunts all over the blocks surrounding the tower, and going straight up was the same as any other route. Besides, their plan was working like a charm so far. Sparkles II didn't sneeze once, and the grunts had already taken notice of him. If anything, things were working out almost too well. Grunts were pouring in from every street and enclosing them on each side. Suddenly, Sparkles II stopped a couple of blocks short of the tower.

The sound of the grunts droning "AWWWW W . . . AWWW . . . AWWWWW . . ." hummed all around them.

"Whoa," said Stan. "That sound is freaking me out."

"Yeah, the grunts like Sparkles II even more than we thought," said Rick.

"I'm going to be hearing it in my sleep—if I can sleep after this," said Stan.

Sparkles II sounded as unnerved as his passengers. "Merrrgh?"

"Awww, Sparkles II, we'll be through the worst part soon," said Rita.

"AWWWWWW! AWWWWWWW!" echoed the grunts.

"Oh, brother," Rick said, shaking his head.

As creepy as the pack of grunts were, they were doing just what they were supposed to. They parted the area surrounding the tower to let their beloved dinosaur pass. It was like a reception line at a grunt wedding. Slowly, Sparkles II was buffeted to the tower. The chorus of AWWWWs grew to an almost deafening roar. The friends made it within two blocks of the tower when Sparkles II stopped again. His admirers held him locked in place, just a few hundred feet shy of their destination.

CHAPTER TEN
FOOL'S GOLD

ACK!" said the mayor-turned-grunt into the microphone, introducing Dr. Dubloon to the crowd of gray-faced citizens. Her disturbing, monotone grunt voice echoed through the streets.

"Why, thank you, Ms. Mayor. It's an honor," said Dr. Dubloon, stepping up to the podium in front of Dubloon Tower. "As a long-time resident of Brickport, it's always been my dream to transform this city to its former glory—and beyond. Well, this is the first brick in the wall, you might say."

Two blocks away, the dinosaur and his team were still stuck.

"MEERRRGGGH!" said Sparkles II, clearly upset. Rita had planned to climb inside once they got close to the tower and then they could all make their way to the front. But Sparkles II was so unnerved and the crowd was so thick that they couldn't move.

"There, there, Sparkles II," Rita said softly.

"Meerrrgh?"

Rita climbed up the ladder and knocked on the door. After a bit of a scuffle, Rick let her inside.

"We can't make it through the crowd," she said. "I think we have to go to Plan B."

"Uh, Plan B?" said Rick. This was the only plan he had.

"There has to be some way to make it through the crowd," said Rita. She found her bag of spare parts and rummaged around in it. Rick put the brick back over the trapdoor.

"Aw, geez, Rita!" he said, exasperated. "What are we supposed to do? Get airlifted to the tower?"

"Great idea!" said Rita. She pulled out the little helicopter Rick had built on the moon.

"Yeah, I mean, of course! What else would we do?" said Rick.

"Good thinking, Genius," said Stan.

With a few enhancements from their bag of tricks, Rick and Rita were able to make the helicopter just powerful enough to lift a Brachiosaurus. Making Sparkles II feel at home in the sky, however, was an impossible task. Rick was at the pedals and Rita hummed a lullaby to their pet. Slowly and clumsily, they made their way over to the podium, just above where Dr. Dubloon was giving his speech.

"MEERRRRGGGH!" Sparkles II bellowed. Down below, the grunts were taking notice. Sparkles II was no less charming to them overhead than he had been on the ground.

"AWWWWW!!!!" chorused the army of grunts.

"What is this monstrosity?" called Dr. Dubloon, startled by the interruption. "And why is it upstaging my ceremony?"

Anyone who could respond to him intelligently was either inside the dinosaur or hiding behind it, so the only response he got was "AWWWWW! AWWWWW!"

"Ah, a dinosaur blimp!" Dubloon said, trying to cover. "Nice touch, Mayor!"

"AWWWW!" said Mayor Grunt.

"He is rather cute, isn't he?" said Dr. Dubloon, momentarily distracted. "Now, where were we?"

"C'mon Rick!" said Rita, looking through the scope in Sparkles II's chest. "We're almost there."

"Rita, can you take over the pedals?" said Rick. "Are you ready, Stan?"

"As ready as I'll ever be," said Stan, looking through the scope one last time. "We're over the podium now. We've got to get down there. Open the door!"

Rick grabbed Rita's bag with the fake Onyx Brick inside. He pulled at the big, awkward piece barring the trapdoor.

"It's stuck," he said.

"I'm sure it'll be fine!" said Stan. "Isn't that what you said?"

Rita pedaled hard, all the while singing to Sparkles II to soothe him. The poor beast was uncomfortable in the sky, and he didn't like what was happening below him, either.

"Meeerrrrghhh."

Stan checked the scope again. "We're going to miss our chance."

Dr. Dubloon was at the podium and about to lay his hands on the real Onyx Brick. Rick was getting desperate. He couldn't let that horrible man win. He pulled harder at the brick holding the door shut.

"With this final brick," said Dr. Dubloon, holding the Onyx Brick high in his gloved hands, "I complete the transition of Brickport to Dubloonville!"

Rick jumped on the door just as Stan pulled the brick free. They tumbled down onto the podium and knocked the Onyx Brick clean out of Dubloon's hands. Stan scrambled after it, disappearing into the crowd.

"Brick! I might have known!" said Dr. Dubloon. "How nice of you to make an appearance. And now if you'll excuse me, I have a ceremony to . . . the Onyx Brick! Where has it gone?"

"AWWWW! AWWWW!" The mayor handed Dr. Dubloon the Brick. But Rick wasn't sure which brick it was, and he had lost track of Stan.

"I thank you, Ms. Mayor," said Dr. Dubloon. "Gentlemen!" Dubloon called to the guards nearby. "Bring Mr. Brick right up front where he can see. That's it!" Dubloon turned back to his captive audience. "Shall we continue?"

"MEEERRRRGGGH!" Sparkles II bellowed. "AWWWWW!"

The crowd of grunts parted, finally making a space for the dinosaur to land.

"Now, Mr. Brick, I have a very special knack for winning people over," said Dr. Dubloon. "If you'll just look into my eyes and touch the Onyx Brick, here."

"No, please! I couldn't. I . . ." Rick's arms popped off just as Dubloon was about to hand him the brick. But Dr. Dubloon was quick. He caught one of Rick's arms and snapped it back in place.

"Keep Mr. Brick calm, would you?" Dubloon told his grunts. Despite his best efforts, Rick could not free himself from their grasp. Dr. Dubloon looked into Brick's face. He spoke to him in that cold, controlling voice Rick heard him use with the mayor.

"That's it, Mr. Brick. Give me your hand."

Dr. Dubloon took Rick's arm and placed it firmly on the brick. But nothing happened.

"I don't understand," said Dr. Dubloon. "Why aren't you changing?"

Rick looked blankly into the distance and tried on his best grunt impression. "Uh . . . UGGGH!"

"Nice try, Brick," said Dubloon. "I don't know why this isn't working, but you won't be able to resist the powers of the Onyx Brick once it's in its place of power!"

Dr. Dubloon raised the door on the bubble covering the niche for the Onyx Brick.

"Welcome to Dubloonville!" cried Dr. Dubloon.

Rick held his breath as Dr. Dubloon lowered the brick into place. He closed his eyes. He plugged his ear with his finger. He held his breath. Then, nothing happened.

"Merrrgggh?" Rick felt a gigantic plastic tongue against his face.

"AWWWWW!!!" went the crowd. Only this time, it sounded different. This time it was heart-felt—human, even. Rick looked around. The gray faces had turned almost completely to yellow, brown, and pink. The sky shone bright blue. As if suddenly realizing they were themselves again, the citizens of Brickport embraced. Rick saw the forlorn father he'd met at the barrier just a few days ago hugging his wife and children. The air was filled with laughter and singing. Even the black tower above them seemed to sparkle.

"This isn't right!" yelled Dr. Dubloon. "The city was supposed to be mine!"

"I'm afraid plans have changed, Francis," said Stan, handing the real Onyx Brick over to the mayor. The mayor held open a sack and Stan dropped it in. Mayor Figg kept her eyes shut tightly and turned her head away, as if avoiding a particularly foul piece of trash.

"But I just . . ." Dr. Dubloon trailed off. He scratched at the brick he had placed in the space created for the Onyx Brick. Beneath a layer of snazzy black paint, a golden hue shone through.

"The old brick-switch trick," Rita said and winked at Rick.

"It's one of my favorites!" said Rick.

"Get Dr. Dubloon!" yelled the crowd. A crowd of former grunts—Dubloon's old security force—surrounded the evil billionaire and carried him through the lively crowd.

"Easy folks," said the mayor. "We are people once again, and we will deal with Dr. Dubloon justly. Officer Mind? Officer Storm?" The mayor addressed two policemen near the podium. They cuffed Dr. Dubloon and put him in the back of a police cruiser. Unfortunately, the cruiser was still missing its tires, so Sparkles II hoisted it up onto his back.

Rick was so captivated by the change in mood, he almost forgot about his missing arm.

"Rick!" said Rita, holding up the limb. "Pull yourself together!" She tossed it to Rick. He managed to pop it back on before scrambling up the ladder and into the dinosaur.

Rick and Rita had a spectacular view through the scope inside Sparkles II's cavernous belly. They made their way to the city jail. The citizens of Brickport formed an impromptu parade behind them. Rick popped a brick out of Sparkles II's spine so he could take a look behind them.

People sang and played drums and guitars. People danced and carried each other. And something else interesting happened. People started building things. They picked up blocks and wheels from abandoned vehicles and rundown structures. They picked up tiny tiles and little coin-shaped studs of every color. Some put together little carts so they could collect pieces along the way. Others made little murals out of the smallest, most colorful bricks. People made little boxes and huts for those who had no place to live. Some citizens made pets—like Sparkles II but smaller—for those living alone so they would have some company. As the parade made its way through the streets of Brickport, the city already seemed to be transforming back to its former glory.

CHAPTER ELEVEN
BRAND NEW CITY, BRAND NEW DAY

After Dr. Dubloon was locked up in the city jail to await his trial, the mayor took the Gold Brick from its place at the base of the tower and locked it up safely in the city vault along with the Onyx Brick so they would never fall into the wrong hands again. Mayor Figg held a ceremony down by the port—far from Dubloon Tower—to honor those who had saved the city. Rick and Rita were given medals. There had never been a city hero as big as Sparkles II, so they had to build a special medal for the dinosaur, which was placed in his chest. It was beautiful: a little round patchwork of blues and pinks and purples and gold. Sparkles II wore it proudly.

Stan didn't make it to the ceremony. He had left the tower just as the parade to the jail was beginning, saying that he felt under the weather. Rick had noticed that he looked a little pale—a little grayer than his usual color. So after shaking hands with the mayor and graciously posing for photos for the *Brickport Gazette*, Rick and Rita took Stan's medal and set off to find him.

It had been only three days since the Dubloon Tower ceremony, but each day seemed to bring more change to Brickport . . . and more inspiration for Rick and Rita. The mayor hired them to rebuild the band shell at the port and to renovate Dubloon Tower to fit their own vision. It was going to be an exciting year for the two architects—and a busy one, too.

Rick and Rita made their way to Starbricks, hoping to find Stan at his usual spot, but there was no sign of him. Rita and Rick talked over their new projects, while Sparkles II soaked up the love of Brickport's citizens. Rita took her cup apart and put it back together. She added little flourishes to it, turning the handle into an animal and making a little flower sprout from the bottom. Then she filled it up halfway and left it for Rick to find. After an hour, they realized that Stan wasn't going to show up.

"He might be really sick," said Rick. "Maybe we should look around for him."

"Do you know where he lives?" asked Rita.

"I didn't think he even had a place to live," said Rick, "but who knows?'

"Should we try the special bathroom?" asked Rita.

"I can't imagine why he would need to use that, but sure," said Rick.

They made their way out the door and up the street. They walked up Rotor and behind Dubloon Tower toward the secret bathroom. They were almost to the door when they saw Stan come out. He didn't see them and crossed to the opposite side of the street.

Rick called out, "Stan!" But Stan didn't stop. Rick called out again. Stan still didn't seem to hear him. But no one could miss Sparkles II.

"MEERRRRGHH!" said the dinosaur. He bounded across the street. A streetlight fell over and some of the plates pulled apart. Rick stopped to fix them while Sparkles II stood blocking Stan's progress.

"Stan!" said Rita, breathless from trying to catch up to their friend. "We've got your medal! How come you weren't at the ceremony?"

Stan laughed uneasily. "Oh! You know, what did I do, really? You two should keep that. You did all the important stuff."

"Are you feeling okay?" asked Rita. "You don't look like yourself."

Stan's face still looked quite gray and his expression was a little dazed. He couldn't seem to meet Rita's eyes and he kept his hands locked securely around his coat.

"You have to take your medal, Stan!" said Rick. "We would never have the Gold Brick without you! Gosh, you don't look so good."

"Why don't you come back to the office with us?" asked Rita. "We'll make you some tea and we can show you our plans for the new tower."

Stan shifted nervously from foot to foot.

"I can't, I'm afraid. I'm have to . . . uh . . . build a new place for myself. I want to finish up before dark. But I'll stop by soon," Stan said. "Very soon! Toodle-oo!"

Then he bolted underneath Sparkles II's neck and made his way up the hill, toward the center of Brickport and the tower. Both Rita and Rick thought he was acting strange, but they were too excited about their plans for the new buildings to think about it much.

If they had been just a little more observant, though, they might have noticed the odd shape beneath Stan's trench coat. It was a very odd shape, indeed, even for a brick. It looked like a brick that would fit one spot and one spot only, and it had just one very big job to do.